T0145140

To order additional copies of this book, contact:
Xlibris
AU TFN: 1 800 844 927 (Toll Free inside Australia)
AU Local: 0283 108 187 (+61 2 8310 8187 from outside Australia)
www.xlibris.com.au
Orders@Xlibris.com.au

ISBN: 978-1-6641-0096-1 (sc)
ISBN: 978-1-6641-0097-8 (e)

Print information available on the last page

Rev. date: 09/18/2020

CONTENTS

CHAPTER 1

Jitter Region, Friendly Start

Ryella Teiran, that was her name, but it wasn't the one that she went by in school, she was known as the top female of the academics' chart in the tenth grade. A short doll-faced teenager with short choppy chestnut brown hair, that looked anything but the type to be high in academics with the messy way she presents herself in the uniform, but the only reason that she knew all of this wasn't due to the studying hard.

The facts she knew were because she repeated in this world many times already, hence knew answers to all the exams many times.

Though, of course, no one knew that was her little secret she kept inside.

Was she going to tell anyone about this little ability she had?

She wasn't quite sure.

Ryella here was changing certain parts in each time she repeats, as the lonely life of just reliving these scenarios over and over again was starting to grind at the back of her mind.

They are agitating that little voice deep within.

So, it was time for a change of pace; hence why she's now venturing onwards to a classroom that was furthest away from the main campus ground. Crossing the restricted gate and taking a look around to the area, she's never been game enough to step in, from the classroom, the halls, and the staff rooms that seem to be empty of people at this present time. Soon she steps out the back gate to where she finds a supply shed and to the right a soccer field bordered by stainless steel fence that stood at about seven feet high.

And on the bleachers to the left of the field was a lone student, sunset red hair that reached to their chin, a handsome baby-faced boy, clad in the general uniform for their academy, less the blazer. Sitting there just leaning back against the seats relaxing in the time he seemed to have alone.

Climbing up to his level, Ryella chuckles before asking, "Skipping too, huh?"

Hearing the words would bring him down to earth and look over his shoulder to her a smile that seems to be plaster to his face. "Oh, you're a fresh face, you're with the main campus students, don't want to hurt your pretty little record staying here."

Rolling her eyes, Ryella swiftly responds with obnoxious; "Please. I can afford the time off. My grades are sky-high."

"Oh? That makes it all the more amusing that you're still over here."

"I don't like obnoxious people."

His eyebrows rose at that, that smile turning into a smirk, "Well since you have free time, feel like entertaining me until my teacher returns?" Rising to his feet and took a step closer to her.

Surprised by request, she thanks herself for taking this short trip here, after all, she just met an interesting boy that is asking for her time, so with a chuckle, she replies with an amused; "Sure, why not, got nothing else better to do while the assembly is going."

Hopping down off the stand, he lands in a crouched position on the dirt, not even taking another glance to Ryella. The boy straightened up and stuffed his hands into his pockets, finally lifting his head to have his molten amber meet with her caramel as he snorts. "Nice, now you like the type that gets knocked down a lot, feel up to fighting me?"

She was dumbstruck, *A fight? Like a sparring session?* Now, this boy spoke her language. "Sure, I'm game,"

Ziro motions come hither, and the redhead would get in position, leading Ryella to the middle of the field, waiting for her to get ready. Carefully, she goes over to him, throwing off her blazer and rolling up her sleeves as she went, leaving at least a three-foot space between them.

He kept his eyes on her, tracking every movement, he didn't want to go easy on her but knew that hurting a girl will stay on his conscience forever and didn't want that. Or did he?

An arch of his brow as she began some simple stretches in front of him, obviously readying herself for the actions ahead; "Don't start crying if you get hurt." He had to comment, or was it more of a warning?

It didn't matter, it still made Ryella stop and slowly look through her hair at him with a smirk growing to her face as she retorts haughtily; "Crying? Hurt? What are you trying to be a bully?"

"You wound me."

She just laughs at him before, grabbing her shoulder and rolling it in preparation, stepping closer towards him, "We'll see if you can land a hit on me."

"A lady with balls, that's a new one, you're gonna be great friends with the man without a dick."

"Do you trash talk you opponent this much it's quite useless on me."

He just laughs at her in return before swatting her hands from him when she was reaching out and taking the first strike only for her take a step back and dodge.

"Is that all you got?"

They would throw fists, kicks, blocks and then slip back to watch each other with grins on their faces. Panting, they would trade their thoughts on their abilities, amazed and amused then would smirk; "No more kid gloves."

He comes running at her before bending one knee to slide under/between her legs to throw a leg up to kick her only to get it caught by hers, and she falls on top of him with a grunt, then laughs hard. He followed suit soon after, patting her back with clammy hands congratulating her for falling for him followed by a; "You wish." From her.

His teacher, Mereki, returned after an hour to stare at the unusual sight in front of him, one of his students, whom he knew had a very peculiar personality, actually speaking lightly with a female student from the main campus. With no threats, no malice, just genuinely enjoying each other's company.

Smiling, the middle-aged man disappears back into the classroom only at the sound of the rest of the students seem to be arriving back, their loud voices echoing over the field.

Hearing those voices, Ryella stops and gets to her feet, telling the boy her goodbyes and walks on back to the main campus to face the music. However, when out of sight, she would see out of the corner of her eye when the boy's classmates came out to see him, they would notice a genuine smile on his face, instead of that smirk his uses.

A short feminine boy with medium blonde hair was the first one to speak out of the group that greeted him, "Something happened?"

"Yeah, got a good workout with a chick from the main campus."

Speckled azure narrowed in the utmost confusion, "The main campus? That's unusual."

"She's new, I think."

"A transfer student? Surely they know how the school system works…"

He shrugs, he didn't care, either way, if she ended up being obnoxious as the rest of their year, he would deal with it. No worries.

CHAPTER 2

Competition

When Ryella saw that boy next, he was jogging down the path from the secluded campus to the main; in quite the hurry, spotting her he began grinning from ear to ear, his rush wholly forgotten when he slowed and walked in time with her through the gates. "Oh, it's main campus chick."

She rolls her eyes at him, shrugging the comment off and making no complaints about him walking with her as she asks; "Skipping again?"

"No, I was running from my teacher for pranking him, so no I'm skipping."

She couldn't help but laugh at him; she could almost see Mereki running after him puffing like a fish, knowing how winded his teacher can tend to get, then when she finally calmed her laughter down, she manages to ask; "Want to skip together?"

"Sure. No one better to hang out with." She snorts before allowing him to grab her hand and hurryingly lead her out of the campus grounds completely around the streets into town, to the arcade, but him being the main one at the games, she just stood to his left most of the day.

"My friend Azuriah, I swear to god, what kind of man has long hair and hips like that!" He would say while coordinating the claw machine to one of the soft toy prizes and mutters a curse when he misses.

Ryella furrowed her brow, seriously is this kid for real to say that about his friend? With a shrug, she went with it; "Just start calling him a ladyboy then?"

There was a pause from him, and she thought maybe that was a little too far, only to be proved wrong by his response; "That was perfect, thank you for that gem." He stops and then just laughs as well as she before they moved onwards to the next game as he spoke. "I know you're new, but you never gave a name."

"Not telling, use that lovely brain of yours to figure out my name from our result charts."

"Yeah, because you easily have good grades to stand out." Sarcasm was dripping in his voice just like last time he spoke about her academic skills.

Smoothly, she crosses her arms as she retorts "I'm second place, Ziro Taylor."

He blinks, she knew his name? Wait that's not the point.

Ryella visibly saw the cogs turn in his head as his expression twists remembering that unusual female name above his rivals', the hilarity of the situation was on hand then but now...

"Holy frick, that's pretty impossible, but you'll never beat me."

"I can surely try."

"Yeah? You haven't yet, so what can you do then, huh?"

Ryella just smirked at the jest and slips over closer, grabbing his wrist, startling the boy who rips his arm in alarm. Pausing from Ziro's reaction, she frowns. Ziro shrugs it off quickly and kicks out a leg to trip her over. Landing on her side like a discarded bag, Ryella just glances up and glares at him, she knew by the smirk that was on his face she has been had.

Ugh, how infuriating this boy can sometimes be.

"You're a dick."

"I know,"

The next time Ryella met up with Ziro, they had run into each other on the weekend, she going out shopping while he was heading over for lunch. A small greeting included before Ryella continued her way.

Stopping when Ziro grabbed her wrist, "...I need a favour."

Eyebrows shot up high, "Excuse me?"

He flushes immediately realising what that sounded like, "No, *no*. Not like that." He pauses, letting go of her wrist when she turned to face him fully, "I have a family thing."

Her eyes narrowed in suspicion, "A *family thing*? Does it include coming over to your own house?"

"No, it doesn't. Oh my god, can you please just ignore how that happened? I'm serious here; I need a date to a dance my relatives always host." He grumbles rubbing the back of his neck, "You're the only girl that approaches me, and Azuriah went last time, *they were not happy.*"

"I'm a fake girlfriend, then?"

"Yes – wait, I mean no! Just *ugh.*"

Ryella just sighs crossing her arms and tilts ahead, "I'll need a few things then, I've never been to...a ball? It's a ball isn't it, please tell me I don't have to wear those huge gowns."

"Y-Yeah, you do."

"Fine, if I'm suffering, you're suffering too."

"Trust me; I'm already suffering."

A roll of the eyes and a small chuckle was received, Ryella then shrugs and agreed. Ziro beamed in relief and grabbed her wrist again, explaining the issues he was going to take care of with her, like dress, shoes, hair and other things she may need.

After what it seems like days, was five hours, the sun was setting, lighting the city in his red and orange hues while the pair sit next to each other on the bus to Ryella's home direction.

Sitting there with bags in their laps, Ziro rests his head in his palm while staring out the window, until he felt an odd weight upon his shoulder, causing him to jolt and look over in alarm.

Ryella had fallen asleep. Her head lolled, resting Ziro's shoulder and clinging the bags, he purchased for her like a lifeline.

Faintly smiling, he rests a hand on her hair and strokes it; "Thanks for dealing with this asshole…" before he soon nods off with his head against the glass.

Ryella's eyes opened slightly once his hand stopped stroking her unruly locks, glancing out of the side to him and sadly smiles; "You're more human than an asshole, Ziro."

CHAPTER 3

Run

Ryella was waiting outside of the secluded campus, the classmates walk outside in groups of three, spotting him being the last out with a male that she assumed was Azuriah because of the strong emphasis on that petite body he had.

And no, he wasn't kidding, she was instantly jealous of those hips.

Their eyes met, and he would stop only to call out to the girl; "Main campus students aren't allowed to step foot in here. More they don't want to."

"I'm here for your friend."

The redhead, Ziro, had already turned to watch his friend Azuriah and Ryella's first interaction before he finally steps over to her with a brow raised only to comment with;

"I'm starting to think you and I may be cut from the same cloth."

"You *thought* we were? How could you, I stalk you for nothing?" Sarcasm was dripping in her voice as she rests her hands on her hips and tilts her head, smirking.

"You and your infatuation with me, I get it, I'm smart and downright hot, but we're fifteen, calm your tits." Crossing arms, staring Ryella down smugly.

Only both to clutch their stomachs in hysteria.

And poor Azuriah stood there watching the pair a little confused and left out.

"This is –"

"Raven, Raven Oliver." She quickly cut him off, speaking the name she was referring to herself as in the many repeats that she had been.

"Finally! The A-class lazy ass gives me a name! Wonder will never cease."

Ryella couldn't help but end up laughing once again at his exaggeration, Azuriah just shook his head before smiling and extending a hand out to her; "Nice to see Ziro getting along with people outside our screwed-up schooling system."

She grabbed it with a brief grip before dropping her hand to the side again, "He can't be all that bad."

"True, it's not, but he can never get along with anyone because he's such an asshole." Ryella just shook her head in return telling the blonde male that he just was too arrogant but knew what he was capable of that's why she understands his personality. It surprised both, only to glance between each other and exchange smiles accepting the girl.

But due to having plans after school already, Ryella just asks if she can join them for the trip until they reached their destination, which was Ziro's home. But they both offered for her to come and study with them. Surprised at the offer, she accepted quite graciously, beginning with the pair into the great big home that Ziro and his family-owned.

Though when they made it up the stairs, Azuriah hesitated to go in because of one reason only. She knew, standing at the doorway to his room and stared as Ziro, not even fazed about this issue, would look back over to Azuriah with a laugh; "I think he forgets I'm a girl."

Ziro held the door open and stared at them with his same characteristic smirk/smile only to snort; "I know you're a girl I just don't care."

"So, he has nothing to hide, oh how does that make a lady want to search his room more."

"You're some crazy chick, Raven."

Azuriah had covered his mouth and was snickering at their arguing that started up before the girl shoved pass them and stepped into his room, boasting about being a teen inside a boy's bedroom and big whoop. Ziro couldn't help but just facepalm at the antics the girl showed before she just suddenly realised…just how *big* his bedroom was.

She was in awe even until they made it up to his bedroom. What kind of kid has a home this big, let alone a room that huge? There were a king-sized bed and a walk-in closet *for crying out loud*. How many gaming consoles were there? Oh wow, that bookshelf to her right was full of encyclopedias, he was an honour student for sure, but an obnoxious and easily distracted one, as well.

Receiving a pat on each shoulder, a boy on each side of her grinning from ear to ear, Ryella couldn't help but recover from her shock to whisper; "God damn rich kid."

Which made Ziro laugh at her and set his coffee table up, unpacking his backpack to get his textbooks out ready for their study session; "Just hit the books."

Said books were open, pens scratching the pages, the notes are written down, the trio was going through each question, that Azuriah had asked to be tutored since he was weak to math. Ryella and Ziro revised the subject while Azuriah is struggling.

"No Azuriah, that's incorrect,"

"But you said the A is equal to X and Y is meant to be the circumference!"

"Yes, but you went in a completely different direction with the answer."

Ziro is amused at Azuriah's disgusted expression that he gave, while Ryella sits there clutching her stomach laughing.

After two hours, Azuriah gave up and flopped backwards onto the carpet with a loud dramatic groan. Leading both Ziro and Ryella dropping pens. Glancing over to the blonde, who is clutching his head, rolling around the carpet complaining about; "My brain about to explode." Smirking, Ziro got up and then moved to the blonde before flopping on top of him when he stopped rolling, and then laughs heartily as the blonde starts to bang fists weakly on his shoulder to get his body off of him.

Ryella watched this with a smile on her face, enjoying watching just how close the pair was.

"That same feeling that you will never get,"

Startled, why was the voice starting to speak now? Ryella bolts up to her feet and grabs her things in a panic, before rushing out quick smart, not even sparing the boys a glance, confusing them both as she just left like that, but she couldn't risk the chance of her sins coming back to haunt her from the previous repeats.

So, she ends up leaving the city for a while.

CHAPTER 4

Return

When she ends up returning to the city in this repeat was around three years after her initial escape, and somehow fate happened to make them walk into each other almost as soon as she settled back in, surprising herself and him.

That once baby faced boy was now a chiselled face, smartly dressed man, with the same red hair in that signature style she knew back when he was in high school, now looking down at her in absolute shock before stammering out; "Wow…um, Oliver, you've …returned?" She could tell he felt awkward speaking to her after she ditched them without another word.

She wasn't expecting them to get along again straight off the bat.

But she tried to, "Yeah, sorry, you look great, though, still making Azuriah jealous about being more manly than he is?"

At the very least; that earnt her a snort/smirk response, breaking the ice. "I'm too badass for Azuriah to catch up."

Ryella pauses for a second, scrunching her face up slightly; "Oh god, please tell me he didn't grow more feminine looking."

"Honestly, no, but he is still short."

She covers her mouth with a snicker imagining the older looking blonde boy at the same height he was in high school. Ziro entirely turns to show she finally has his attention before just dropping the ball and asking; "What gives Oliver? You just suddenly looked scared all of sudden and then I don't see you again for *three years*, what the hell would have brought that on?"

Ryella glanced away, rubbing her arm sheepishly. This *thing* of hers wasn't something that a human would understand; she knew that much. Though had to figure out how to explain without sounding, absolutely insane, so with a sigh, she quickly came up with; "It's *tough* to explain, I owe you one at least, so just believe me when I say; I needed to get out of here quick."

Though Ziro wasn't happy with the explanation, he dealt with it with a shrug; "*Fine.*"

She offers to try at least to catch up as much as possible, which he accepted as he was on his way home from work, either way, hence their conversation-starting shaky but returning to what it was before she left as soon realised she never changed at all. Once the ice finally broke, he offers her over, since Ziro's parents are never around.

Accepting the offer without hesitation, as they were both adults, coming into that familiarly large house and bedroom, sitting around at the coffee table while he grabbed drinks she just looks around and saw that nothing had changed except for a few sports trophies and more photos. But what surprised her was there was a photo of her with him. Wait, she was asleep, was that on the bus home from their time skipping class together? *He had a photo of her on his collection of memories?* She felt the heat rise to her cheek, and in her chest, it was a new feeling, the fact that Ziro held her that close without even being that close to him. "Looks like I was wanted around after all."

Ziro finally returns, Ryella was close to the memorial that lies on his wall of every friend and event that has happened. Ziro was surprised when she had taken the photograph of her and him away as well as one of him and Azuriah when they had started their first year of high school. Both decent and happy images that he held dear. "You were out like a light, but you looked to be having a nightmare…it was still adorable." He explained, slipping down to sit next to her on the floor while she surfed through his pleasant memories.

"You're an odd man, Ziro Taylor."

"Hm?"

"No person ever wants to have anything to do with an unstable person like me." She whispered under her breath, staring down at the nostalgic item.

But of course, that caught his attention; "Unstable? You haven't seemed unstable to me unless there is a psychological thing going on." He hesitated in asking the last part, as he was aware that it was a sensitive subject.

"Well, it's not psychological, but there is *a thing.*"

Ziro decided to leave that alone, understanding that it's a possibility it was hard to talk about, and he knew she'd tell him when she was ready. Pinning them back up in their retrospective spaces, she sits at the table, and they create a good conversation before she even ended up staying the night, but his suggestion, of course.

Which leads to the awkward stage of; "*Where the hell was she going to sleep?*"

Ziro blinked when she actually said that out loud, and just dismissively replied; "My bed, isn't that obvious? It's big enough."

So Ziro wasn't fazed by an actual woman was going to be in his bed now, is he? "Ziro, you have to realise *I am a girl.*"

"I am aware that you have tits. That means nothing; it's just sharing a bed,"

Okay, Ziro left that open, by damn, Ryella took that chance to tease him. "Oh, so you've been staring at my boobs now, huh?"

Ziro just grabs a pillow and throws it at her in retaliation, *"Oh my god,"* a small little childish moment was something she's going to cherish in the back of her mind….

Ryella laughs, Ziro shakes his head with a roll of the eyes, guiding her to where she could change. Gives Ryella some of his clothes before retired for the night and got settled in the bed. Backs to each other, Ziro had quickly settled down and dozed off, Ryella would slowly roll over to gaze upon his full return and whisper; "Even if I told you what was wrong with me, you'd never believe me…" then dozes off into a dreamless sleep.

And when Ziro awoke, he would notice the bed on the side that Ryella was sleeping on was empty. Frowning, he would rub his eyes groggily and heave his body out of bed onto to spot a note on top of his phone, which was her address and number.

That frown turning back into his signature smile/smirk, he went along with the morning like usual.

CHAPTER 5

Bonding

That bonding circumstance allowed both Ryella and Ziro to keep in contact, and even meeting up frequently, whether it was discussing his job and daily antics within, or just enjoying each other's company.

Now and again, Azuriah would join in their meeting, his appearance was another refreshing thing to see after everything, and even slip into routine conversations, and spilt about high school to Ryella.

The next time they all met was when Ryella officially settled into her home again. She invited Azuriah and Ziro for a small party, or rather, just a general get together. However, Azuriah asks to bring their girlfriends' Jasinta and Emilie over, much to Ziro and Ryella's surprise.

"Hold on, you *both* have girlfriends now? Why not tell me?"

Azuriah glances to Ziro a little taken aback by this, before since she had returned and even pulls a sceptical expression when the redhead just glances away from him quickly trying to avoid the subject like homework.

"To be honest, I thought that you and Ziro's relationship was borderline you having a crush on him at high school until you just vanished." The blond explains sighing and a minor shrug, trying to dismiss it

Silence followed from that before they hear Ziro grumbling to Azuriah that; "Wasn't something to approach now."

Though Ryella just rolled her eyes and smiles. Appreciating them trying, but soon frowns realising in the back of her mind that, *they thought she had fallen for the redhead?* "Wait, back up… I never even showed any interest in Ziro in that way ever…? We were just friends?"

"Wait. So, we read that wrong the entire time?"

"No, you're the only one that read that situation like that Azu, I didn't care."

"Enough. It's fine! Forget about it now guys. It's okay really," She chuckles trying to stop the fight that she knew was about to break out by stepping between the two, "Bring them with you, I don't mind, I'd love to meet such ladies' that stole your hearts while I was gone." Followed by a cheeky grin, and the boys relaxed instantly.

That's what ended up happening, the two boys – no men grabbed their phones and quickly got to contacting their partners to see if they were available, led to them turning up last minute to Ryella's apartment in a mad rush. The dishevelled looks of the two females made Ziro laugh and tease, while Azuriah was in front of his partner helping her in a panic to be decent again.

Once the men moved to the sides of the respective woman, introductions made, Emilie was the one that had captured Ziro's heart, a pretty petite Caucasian woman with chocolate hair that reached to her hips in a side braid. While Azuriah's partner, Jacinta, was a tall slim woman of African heritage, with dyed straight blonde hair like him.

Ryella was in awe, resting her chin on the couch back staring at the two women, a stabbing pain now filling her chest, she did feel happy for them, really she did, beautiful woman that treat them well.

Not like how she could, no human, no creature would accept her fully, and Ryella knew.

But why did it hurt so much?

Shaking her head quickly when her name called, she introduced herself to them and showed them around. Ordering takes out and drinking some cheap beer with them, or Ryella was just drinking a little too much.

Seeing that she was out of commission Azuriah called it a night, taking his partner with him, while Ziro did the same.

Though, Ziro returns to Ryella apartment. He was deciding that, after walking Emilie to the nearest train station, of course. Then shucks off his coat, hanging it on the rack, leaving the pair in the spacious and now quiet apartment, for the night.

Ryella was resting on the couch with eyes closed and an arm draped over her face as he came to the conjoined living room. Chuckling, Ziro leans over the sofa back, looking down to her and peel that arm off her eyes, only to be startled and drop the limb in fright when her eyes just stared back at him.

Catching the limb before it hit herself in the face, she let out a dry chortle and sits up to lean over the furniture that she perched on, and glances up to him.

"A little voice in my head keeps telling me things.." She suddenly began giggling her head off and slips back to her original posture on the couch, while the redhead just stood there a little dumbstruck.

What was she talking about, what did that even mean?

Was she way too drunk to take seriously now…right?

Ziro watches her in slightest concern, before slipping around to pick up the discarded glasses from their earlier group session, only to pause when he bent down and sees her turning to her side to watch him with a keen eye.

"It's the reason I had to leave when I did…" Her flushed face and hazy eyes from her alcohol consumption were in his view and the reason why he didn't take her as dangerous as she seems at this present moment.

"So *that's* why, you listened to some weird little voice that's making decisions for you, huh?" He smirks, thinking that this was going to be the best thing to tease her about later.

Only to stop and stare at her gobsmacked as she retaliates with; "Yeah, because I'm weak and can't control the voice's impulses… I'm the Déjà vu after all…"

When her eyes met with Ziro's once more, everything that he felt, she saw, just that whirlpool of many emotions that were coming to the surface as they spoke, the few she was utterly familiar with were, *betrayal, anger and fear.*

They were everything she had seen over and over again.

Finally gaining the courage to speak, a quiver in his voice, chuckling weakly; "That's in bad taste to joke about that, Oliver."

She just stares at him long and hard, making him slowly come to terms with it and shakily sighs; "It… explains how you say you're unstable…"

Quickly looking away from Ryella and glares at the floor, Ziro was angry at himself, for he never realised it. "So, everything you do is just a game to you?"

She froze, the rest of them just looks at her expectantly instead of staring off the ground, at the same time, readying herself for what to do next. Slowly lifts her head, glancing over her shoulder, coming to terms of what was ahead of her. The repeating of time over the exams spared her from this hurt and the humans from interacting with her. She just merely wanted to keep them safe from the many little voices in her head that were threatening to take over. "None of this is a game …it's always a curse." She then fully turned around to face them before saying with a sad smile; "I felt like I was normal around you lot…until now when reminded of this curse…"

Taking a need breath, she then says one last thing; "*Jitter Region: Reload.*"

Startling the others that were with her, which lead to Ziro's eyes bulging and darting over to get a grip on her as he screams out in devastation and panic; "Hang on, *wait*! Ryella, don't!"

But his cry fell to deaf ears as she suddenly falls from sight into nothingness.

CHAPTER 6

Demonic

Blinking the flickering white from her eyes and find herself back hanging out the gates of the main campus, and by the sight of the many gathering students, she assumed it being assembly day. Making her way through the crowds to her respective class area, she would notice to her left the secluded classroom students she knew so well, yet the sharp stabbing pain at sight.

When the redhead glanced over in her direction with a slightly curious expression on his face, as if he felt someone's eyes upon him, Ryella never even bothered converse or even acknowledge them. She only watches out of her preferential vision him shrug it off and turn straight back to Azuriah and spoke, before laughing at the blonde's expression.

"Oh look at them, so happy...and here you are..."

Ryella's eyes widened, the voice in the back of her head spoke. Lucky being back of her class lines and rushed out before even being noticed through the halls. Venturing off in the direction to the secluded campus, trying to run away from this voice she had that was beginning to scare her.

Ryella couldn't help but feel all of her sins start to crawl down her back in this moment.

Especially when she came face to face with the new face of a straight-laced middle-aged man, standing at the doorway as if waiting for the students to return. Spotting her, he tugs the cigarette that was sitting between his lips and says; "Surely you main campus students have better things to do than snoop about during class."

Red, that's the gradient growing in Ryella's vision as the whispers that voice started again.

A lone chuckle surprised her, as he slowly smirks, noticing the hostility now beginning to flow from the 'student' in front of him. "The Déjà vu never thought I'd see the day you'd show your face to a military."

Ah, minor relief and fear flowed through her veins as he mentioned that name. He knew the legends about her powers. But did he see the state that could become because of them...?

If so, she needs to ask, him and quickly.

"I maybe, but I need you to do something for me."

That seemed piqued his interest enough to butt his cigarette and cross his arms over his chest to show her she has his full attention. "I'm all ears, Ryella Oliver."

After her conversation with the man, Heath, she found out; she came back to the field on which she first met Ziro in that previous reload, and hovered around before perching herself at the front bleacher just waiting.

And when the morning assembly came to a close, and she overheard the bustling of the other teenagers in the distance, signalling them returning to their designated classrooms, she suddenly thought over about Ziro and trying to converse with him again.

You know, maybe start fresh?

"He never liked you, to begin with, he was just acting; it was all an act to get you to entertain him."

But no, starting fresh was a wrong move, gritting her teeth and clenching her fists, she felt it coming hard, *and she knew she couldn't stop it.*

"Excuse me, are you okay?"

Ryella whipped around when Mereki happened to come outside to her, concern written on his face, his soft voice only temporarily breaking her away, before her expression concerted into a panic. "Hurry, *leave now!*"

"He is just showing you pity, why would he care about you? You're a curse."

With a gasp, clutching her head briefly, she felt a snarl ripple from her throat, before she suddenly lurches forth hands wrapping around his throat tightly. His hands were desperately clawing at her hands to pry them away to no avail, slamming her knee to his stomach, making both him and her lose balance and land to the ground.

Mereki's hands try in a desperate attempt to grab hers to stop her at any means. "Stop! Fight it!"

But the words didn't puncture her this time, as it had fully taken over her subconscious. And with that, she tightened her grip upon Mereki's throat and watched him wheeze and lips turn blue at the lack of oxygen in his system.

"Looks like I got to you first, dear old Mereki."

"If...that...makes you...happy..."

She watched his lips move to mouth something which caused Ryella's eyes to widen, the dread pitching into her, before she looks at her hands in fear, shakily reaching down to cup the teacher's face before she let out a pitched scream.

"Enough of that. Mereki didn't mean anything to you, nor did the little brats."

Her scream was cut short into a maniacal laugh, returning to her feet before moving to the supply shed, grabbing an axe that was sitting on the shelf for the gardening group, and grins wildly as the voices of students came closer.

The next targets were coming.

A smirk came to Ryella's face, watching the teens stand there frozen in fear, even as much as they wanted to run, they couldn't.

Giving Ryella the chance to run and slaughter all except for Azuriah and Ziro, that pleaded, for them to stop. To no avail, especially as Ryella kicks Azuriah down and then grabs Ziro to place the blade of the axe to his throat; *"Silly brat, this only happened because of you."*

Ziro widened his eyes, tears rolling down his cheeks, a forced smirk crept to his face; "Only a monster would blame their insanity on someone else." The blade sliced through his throat and she watched him flop to the ground the splatters of red falling on himself and on his friend who was watching him—desperately hoping that this was all a bad dream.

Ryella smirks down at the blonde boy, before moving down to kneel in front of him; "Once I reload, you will watch your friends die over and over again until I'm satisfied,"

"Y-You're a monster! Inhumane!"

"Do you have the balls to do anything about it?"

Azuriah quickened breaths were the only response she received; the boy turned around to crawl away from the girl, his hair all of sudden bein grabbed and tugged on, the axe thrusts right into his back and pulled out quick smart. She was satisfied at the mess she had made and moved again, carelessly swinging that axe. Humming in tune in her amusement, venturing to each target that stood in front of her in her path.

"No stop! This isn't what I want!" Ryella was suddenly breaking free for a moment, as she grips the handle of the axe hard, stilling as her whole body trembles as she realises something about herself; *I never really had any humanity, to begin with.*

"I always knew you were a vile creature in disguise, Oliver."

Struggling to stop her hands as they pose ready for battle, she knew another bloodbath was to come, just as she knew that many are coming soon, but Ryella knew deep down inside that Heath was the only one that will break the cycle she is making in this repeat.

No. In this *Reload*.

"You can't slaughter every human being and then reload."

He was calm/stoic as usual, watching her every movement, readying himself for her next attack, she just cocks her head to the side before stepping forward to him smirking.

"Stop! Please! No more blood on my hands!"

Again, Ryella paused to curse and grab her head only to raise it and look to Heath with her face holding half the saddened and half the crazed expression.

"Defeat that monster inside of you before you come back, Déjà vu." Heath could see the visible inner torment and walked closer to her before resting the barrel of his gun against her chest, the sound of the gunshot echoed in both their ears, the girl falling before disappearing in an abundance of glittering dust;

"Restart."

CHAPTER 7

New Region, Sora

When the black across her vision finally cleared, Ryella would have to sit up slowly, opening eyes as she sees herself on a bed in this unfamiliar room. Dress with a bedside table to her right, a desk in the far left corner near the door that was ajar, caution settled in for a moment; "Is this how I'm starting this new world...?" She closed her eyes to try and think about what happened in the last world.

Only to cringe, as everything flashed throughout her mind at once, and to try and dismiss it for the meantime she dots up from the bed, though was glad that she felt a little more in control right now, she knew it was going to happen again eventually.

After all, that voice never stops telling her pretty little lies and reminding her of her sins to follow.

"I am scared of my existence, but it seems that...nothing can stop me..." Covering her face, she then took a deep breath. Gaining the courage, she would move to exit the room she was occupying, to be met with a tall Asian ethnic woman with long black hair, clad a green polo shirt and black pants, in the small kitchen just opposite the doorway of the bedroom.

She would turn and greet them; "Morning, since you're awake, take a seat, breakfast will be ready in a sec!" Ryella did just that, sat down at the table while the woman continued; "I saw you passed out on the streets. Sure, ...it might be dangerous for me to bring a stranger into my home, but...you covered in blood."

Ryella was worried at that comment, did her load system not work anymore? Can she die in this world? Confused, she decided to just listen to the woman in front of her.

"But there seemed to be nothing on you but the blood once I cleaned you up."

That answers that.

Nodding, she watched the woman place down a plate with toast and fried eggs, confused; she glances over to the woman in front of her about to question the two servings of food. Only for her to beat her to it; "For you, you look like you need it, so go for it."

She was a little hesitant but then ended up slowly eating the food that was in front of her, savouring the food as tears began to roll down her face. The other woman just moved to sit down in front of her with a sad smile on her face; "You got a home to go back to?"

Ryella just shook her head, hanging it in shame and clenching her fists; "I've been in so many places now, I don't even remember which one was my real one..." it was the truth, with all the drama of that little voice. She's never had the time just to sit there and figure out ...where she came from before the Jitter Region.

The woman in front of her just opened her mouth to say something, only to decide against it and just ate her food in silence, the clicking of the fork hitting the plate echoing in the silence. After breakfast, Ryella ends up taking the dishes to the sink, washing them and sitting them on the rack to dry, before glancing over to the other woman; "Do you mind, and I clean myself up also?" After all, she's beginning to feel a slight ache in her joints, whether it was from the time she passed out or the jump into this new world.

Gaining a dismissive wave and an affirmative answer from her, Ryella asked and followed the directions to the bathroom, pushing the door close behind her and gingerly steps over to view herself in the mirror. She touches her face tracing the worn-out indentations that were her cheeks, and trace down her throat and prominent collarbone. Then tugs at the collar of the shirt she seemed clad in, a sweater that was a few sizes too big for her, it was slipping down one shoulder, that belonged to the woman she was sure, as it made her look much smaller than what she was. "I'm still brunette, though." She let out a snort at that, though couldn't even remember what she looked like before her first restart.

Cleaning up, she would take a towel and rub her hair dry as she walks out to meet up with the woman again; "Sorry, I've got to run to work, you can stay here if you want, just rest up okay! I'll be back soon!"

Was this woman going to let a stranger stay in her home? She can't be that naïve can she? Ryella thinks to herself with a sigh, glancing around the doorway and watches Shizu run out of the apartment, echo of the door slamming. *She is,* she just shrugs and returns to the bedroom and just started to take some notes down about this world before she forgets.

CHAPTER 8

Nightmares

It is everywhere.

That one colour she hated so much.

Red.

She stands there staring at her hands in absolute shock, eyes wide as an owl's but vision blurry as if she was underwater. Her voice just croaked out a few sounds before breaking into sobs. The whole area was chanting out what she had done wrong, only *one mistake,* and it was a fatal one. No one can believe that she did something so vile. Two faces stared down at her, one of the faces looked white as a sheet, fear wafting off them in waves and the other one with a look of guilt and desperation.

Please someone, just tell me it is only just a huge nightmare, that I didn't do this! Not again!

Once more that little voice in the back of her head made her go insane, red dripping from her fingertips, clothes and even her face. The weapon that caused the deed shakily held in between her hands; this never meant to happen; it was her idea to live normally, be human.

But that damn ability, the Déjà vu.

It was a curse, not a gift.

Ryella bolts up with a gasp, hand to her sweat coated face; the room felt way too hot, her throat was closing up, making it hard to swallow.

That voice in the back of her head, was that the Déjà vu talking?

Or is it something that lives inside her conscious?

Shaking her head, she got up to look at herself in the mirror before widening her eyes at the reflection she was met.

Whatever it was, it was in her body of this world staring back at her with a crazed grin and glowing red eyes whispering with a knife in hand;

"You can never stop me."

Ryella let out a scream before falling to her knees and clutching her head, chanting out 'no's and 'I don't want to kill anyone!'. She thought that with how loud her voice was Shizu would come running into her room looking at her in concern. Wait, Shizu was still at work, she should've realised that.

God, she felt pathetic to rely on the poor innocent mortal.

Shaking her head, she darts from the room to the front door to open it, slipping out of it, locking it from the inside for the human's security, deciding not to even leave a trace behind before she left the apartment building.

Sighing as she walks out to the street and glancing around at the city/town she was now in, in this world. She then passes some mortals while walking, but there was a strange feeling as she went past, but she shook it off, and shrugged onwards, only for a hand to grab her wrist. Surprising her, Ryella glances over her shoulder to the one that caught her; it was a girl with bubble-gum colour haired, that was smiling brightly at the sight of her and that dark hoodie, jeans and beanie. Staring down at the girl, Ryella looked at her, confused, "Hey! Care to come with us to the arcade?"

Was everyone this naïve in this world? My god. Ryella thought to pull a face of disgust, ripping her arm free before retorting; "Go back to school, you stupid brat."

Oh god, she realised. Was that the voice in the back of her head talking again. Is it taking over her yet? Or was that her saying that?

She felt scared and quickly moved off, leaving the bubbly girl staring at her confused, her friends coming up to her and asking questions of concern. Ryella grits her teeth, no more relationships, friends or family, she needs to own everything on her lonesome.

Hopefully, nothing wrong will happen.

But something does. It always does.

CHAPTER 9

Research

Finding the city library, swiftly searches through the non-fiction, history books more so. Then perches at one of the lounges hidden at the back of the aisle and began reading some books just to learn more about the world and thinking over the differences between the last one.

Sighing, as her brain received too much information at once, she leans back, resting the book over her face and lean back in the sofa, slowly falling asleep.

Only to be woken up by hand shaking her shoulder what seems a mere few moments later, though it was in actual a few hours later. Pulling the book away from her face, she would meet a smiling young, flawless faced, green-eyed, straw-haired male clad in a sweater, apron and long black pants looking down at her. "Sorry ma'am, but we're closing, we need you to leave."

Oh, time to wander the streets some more, she then moved to collect the books that she had read and proceed to put them back.

"Whoa, did you read all those?" he gazes down to three different piles of books balancing on each other, then over to Ryella, who was in the middle of collecting one heap at a time to return to their designated homes on the shelves.

"Yeah, call it, wanting to refresh knowledge," she mumbles in return glancing over to him as he collected one other pile and followed behind her

"They're all non-fiction though, do you just like facts?"

"History is a strong suit of mine."

"Really? Even the magical ones?"

"I guess they intrigue me," She mumbles in return, finally placing the last one back on the shelf and looks at him. Seeing him practically sparkling in admiration, and then splutters out in his excitement; "My friends and I have this thing happening at my place, do you want to join."

"I prefer not to intrude." She responds curtly, trying to cut the conversation short.

"We're not all bad, come on; it'll be fun! You've been studying all this time, how about some relaxation?"

She hesitated, but because he insisted, and it was evident that they were both legal age, she agreed and followed him down the street once he locked up the council property. When arriving at this large vintage cottage, the boy would unlock the door to let her in first, cautiously she would look around while listening to the loud voices that echoed through the home.

It was cosy, warm and full of friendly faces.

Ryella couldn't help but smile genuinely at the sight when the man came up to his friends, one with long black hair wrapping an arm around his neck to pull him down, but when her eyes came upon a familiar face, she blanches.

Oh shit, it was that bubble-gum girl.

"Oh, you're the one from before! Hey, I'm Utau nice to meet you!"

…Huh? Wasn't she mad? Jesus Christ, this region, it was weird.

But the shining in her eyes and her extended hand, made Ryella think maybe she could work with this, no one will find out. "Nami…Nami Aura…" She had to work out a name to use in this world, but she felt satisfied with the one she came up with on the spot, reaching her hand out to shake the girl's, receiving a bright smile in return.

She then was introduced to the rest of the group that was there, the raven-haired boy, slim and lean build with a long-sculpted face, whom just nods his head to her with a mumble of; "Mizuki," as his crimson laced brown eyes stared directly into hers.

Then the boy that brought her to his home just brings in some drinks and offering his name too; "Murasaki,"

Ryella nods before taking a cup and chattering along with the group just general small talk, more on their side than hers as she just sat there, sipping drink after drink while listening. Before too long, she had way too much to drink and was not even able to work out what was real or in her head.

"Look, they're making fun of you."

She just laughs at the voice in her head, no worries on her shoulders right now for the first time in so long; "No, they're not, silly little demon voice, I'm perfectly fine here! Chill out!" As if it was someone trying to create conversation out loud, she exclaims. But it wasn't just her laughing; it was Mizuki and Utau who were so confused at whom she was talking to but didn't care, it was entertaining to watch, as well as funny.

Murasaki ended up being the only one that didn't have anything to drink and was sitting there watching everyone, making sure they were behaving themselves. Still, when Ryella began to speak like that and turn to look like she was having a conversation with nothingness, he decided it was time to get her to stop. "All right Nami, you can stay here tonight, take my bed for the night."

A hiccup and a giggle followed her response; "God…y-you mortals are naïve! The evil little demon voice tells me that you're too easy to manipulate! We could kill you where you stand!"

"Nami, that's a wild imagination you have." Quite frankly, Murasaki was a little worried at such a statement but decided against better judgement to let the girl into his room and eased her onto his bed to watch her curl up giggling.

Turning to leave her for now, she reaches out to grab the hem of his shirt to watch him and then asks; "The Déjà vu is confused."

He pauses just for a moment, "Hm? You mean the legend of the world jumper…?"

"Yes! That's what the evil little voice inside my mind is! It's the Déjà vu curse!"

"I see, so you're the Déjà vu then?" Murasaki hesitated just a small bit when asking that, though staring down at the now drunk woman, he just shakes his head, no way in hell she would be that vulnerable if she wanted to slaughter anyone of them.

"Yup!"

"Interesting fact, thank you for telling me."

Ryella rolls over on the bed to look up at him through her hair, "You're not scared?"

"Not at all." He offers her a small smile, watching the flushed face of the girl consort into confusion at the fact that he didn't show any senses of fear at all. Ryella then felt hot tears well up in her eyes before she closes them and let out soft, pathetic sobs letting go of him, which he took and left the room—closing the door softly behind him, before staring hard down the stairs to his friends that were having a decent time without him.

Murasaki didn't lie, he wasn't scared of her, but he was slightly worried just what she was capable of, he's only heard the legends, but he knew.

All of them could handle this beast in disguise.

Breaking his thoughts by hearing Mizuki calling out from the living room where Murasaki had left them; "Mura, come back down! We're playing truth or dare!"

"Coming, coming!" He returns to them recovering that big old smile for his friends as he spent the rest of the night with them.

When morning came, Ryella woke up with a slight throbbing in her head. Soon it vanished before she shook her head and got up rubbing her head, looking around to where she crashed, to realise that she was in Murasaki's bedroom, heaving her substantial body up she then carefully made her way out of the door to find the young man.

Which she did, he was outside her room holding a tray of food and drink, with some Tylenol on the side? Oh right, mortals get hangovers.

She shook her head before reaching to rub her head; "Nah, I'm good, normally goes away in a few hours if I sleep,"

"You really should at least drink more-"

"Worry about your friends more; I'm not one of them remember?"

He pauses, surprised at her outburst, but the serious look on her face told him that she didn't forget what she said last night so the discussion he was slightly nervous on having begun with; "I see, so… you are them, huh?"

"Yes…but lately I've realised that the Déjà vu is a part of me, but not… me…"

"Hm? That's why you kept saying the evil voice in my head? Is something also taking residence there?"

"…That's what I'm guessing. I don't ever wish to hurt anyone, but they take over, when I'm mentally weak, or something like that…"

"Ah, so when you're emotionally and mentally unstable, the little voice in your head decides to make a move and ends up killing people?"

She cringes, she knew it sounded insane, but it was all she could put it down.

Sighing, Ryella just moves to pass the man to walk down the stairs. Seeing his friends all passed out in random places with blankets over them, she smiles sadly at the sight of them. Only to feel a hand on her head from the man she was just speaking to; "We don't scare away that easily, Nami, you're still welcome here whenever. Now, I'll give you a lift home,"

That made things hard, she didn't have anywhere she was staying, but she could return to Shizu's, maybe apologise for leaving like that. But she wasn't sure it was a good idea at the moment. So, she shook her head, which made Murasaki frown, and looks at her confused only to cut off as she replies with; "I guess you could say, I'm new in town."

"Oh, you only arrived in this world recently?"

"…Yesterday."

He snorts; "Wow. Don't hold a good cover, do you?"

"Well…I spent a good few years in my previous world without anyone finding out until it attacked." Ryella heaved out a sigh and looked down to her hands; "Honestly, I don't deserve to hide for everything that I've done."

He sighs, before glancing over to his sleeping friends and then smiles, before looking over to her telling her; "You can stay with me if you have nowhere to go, as I'm *not afraid of you.*" Ryella agreed, and he told his friends when they woke up. But deep down, she felt a little odd about how Murasaki took this information so easy being a mortal.

Or maybe he wasn't one.

CHAPTER 10

Suffering

After a few weeks, Ryella stood in front of the door that she remembers being where Shizu stayed, or rather where she escaped, her hand hovering over to knock on the door before lowering it and then turning to race off from the building. Straight down the street and back into the library where she stayed once more. Flipping through books, reading different magazines, and even writing a few notes to herself.

"no one is noticing us…"

Ryella felt this cold shiver strike her back when she heard that and then whipped around wildly, unsure how to handle that. But, Murasaki comes out from one of the counters. Started to stack the books she had already read up, smiling down to her; "Reading again, huh?"

"Got to remember, I fall into different worlds with no connections or idea what this world is …so, that's why I study a lot."

"That makes sense."

Ryella looks up, meeting Murasaki's smile again. She didn't say anything else to him, just helping him stack the books back, because she knew if he was immortal or *whatever* the little voice in her head would tell her everything about it.

He was human, which was more than she could say about herself.

Sighing, she throws him a smile when she finished packing up and then moved to leave. He would just nod to her and watched her go before returning to the desk. But when she was walking on the street, everything was crumbling down on her.

Even though she looked reasonably typical, Ryella was tired; she's hardly slept or eaten, she was having trouble keeping up with everything that goes on around this world, let alone work out to keep herself alive here. Usually, when she's thrown into a world, she relies on people around her, but she was trying not to do that to make sure that the Déjà vu curse doesn't overtake her.

And it was just as her consciousness was falling when two familiar people spotted her and came racing over to help; "We can't take her to the hospital! Mizu, she has to go to Mura!"

"Jesus, did she try to starve herself to death?"

"*Hurry!*"

CHAPTER 11

Magic

"How stupid can you get? You think that suicide will make this go away?"

Ryella lies there in the dark, eyes welling up with tears; she felt herself just spinning around in circles, making her think dizzyingly overwhelmed.

"No one will care if you die, either way, that's why they must pay."

She closes her eyes again, smiling slowly until the blackness just vanishes with white until her eyes open and she would find her lying in a bed, rugged up under soft blankets, comfortable.

Glancing around with lidded eyes, she still felt exhaustion and just sitting up was hard for her, a small hand grabbed hers, and she glances over to see who it was; "Hey, you looked like you had it rough…we had reasons not to take you to the hospital so…we've been keeping an eye on you…"

It was that bubble gum girl…what was her name again? Right, Utau. That was sweet of her to do that, but she didn't feel like it was worth anything. Especially when her body already healed. It was just; her mental state was in the wrong way.

And that was scaring her more.

"Thanks…" She manages to croak out, her hand twitching under the other girl's pulling it slowly from the grip, even though her body screamed to leave it there for any sort of skin to skin contact.

"We brought you to Mura's because you knew where he lived, you were on the brink of starvation…" Utau went quiet for a while before looking away. Then back over to her again and whispering to her; "Black magic…huh?"

She snaps her attention straight over to the girl who was now sheepishly smiling like she figured out a deep secret all on her own.

"We use magic too."

"How did you find out…?"

Utau had moved to her feet and the door, hovering as she glances back at Ryella; "It's pretty obvious…"

Ryella let out a dry laugh and looked back to the bed and squeezes the covers in her hands; "I am always pretty obvious, huh?"

"No, Murasaki told us." She looks to her one last time with a smirk and darts out, as Ryella sat there stunned that she used a joke at this time.

What is with these people, Seriously.

An hour later, Mizuki was the next person to come through the door, glancing down at the girl with a cold stare, crossing his arms and leaning against the doorframe; "So, Utau says you're a black magic user."

"Wow, news travels fast even when I want it to be a secret, I'm terrible at keeping things, aren't I?"

"You are." Mizuki looks to her with a half-smirk and chuckles at his reply. Sitting up again, wrapping the covers around her body tightly, while she was in the middle of the bed, keeping warm, watching the male. He would sigh before uncrossing his arms; "Look, we get it,"

"Get what?"

"The voice in your head."

That surprised her; he gets it? How? He is only mortal and never has experienced something like this?

"I can only vouch for my experience. Though Utau can tell you otherwise, normally the other voice inside one's mind that doesn't sound like your means that there is something else that is possibly inside of you, like a spirit trying to use your body as the host."

"Wait, possessing? That's a wild theory there…"

But the look on Mizuki's face told her he was outright dangerous, that there was no lie or joke behind it.

A spirit could be controlling her at her weakest.

Finding out that…it was another being that had taken residence in his own body, it made a few things click in her mind. Wait…there could be something, possessing her?

Before she realised it, she had fallen into the pit of darkness again.

CHAPTER 12

Voices

Stress was high; she could hear the voice inside her head speaking up even more than it used to, saying; *"They're all lying, they don't understand anything, they don't like you. They are making fun of you…"*

Ryella couldn't handle staying with Murasaki much longer even if it was until she was feeling better, they were friendly people. She didn't want to risk the case of the Déjà vu curse taking over, finally, after two months of being in that world again, staying with Murasaki and just holding on by a thread, so when it became quiet within the home. She got out of there as quickly as she could, gathering her things and tiptoeing her way out managing to bump into Shizu, who was staring at the girl that looked a little worse for wear but frowned; "You disappeared."

Ryella avoided Shizu's gaze, fist clenched tightly, flashes of her vision appearing in her mind, reminding her, what she has done. But she gave a false smile still looking away and replied with, "Sorry, I didn't feel comfortable there…"

"I liked you here though; I didn't mind you staying…"

Ryella's smile faltered, and her skin started to feel slightly clammy, how did this woman think such a thing? Was she just a lonely human? Did she understand who Ryella was? Or was she just outright stupid? They knew each other for an hour, and this was getting excruciating.

"Please, can we just get to know each other?"

Her fist tightened, the fight within her mind began to be unbearable as she tried to hold it together without the other woman noticing.

"Hey?"

All of Ryella's fears were coming down right on her…she was hoping that her abilities weren't on show in this world, that the little voice in the back of her head would let her live a healthy life here and never have to tell Shizu, especially after she had given her a home here, the first night she came.

She was only human, and Ryella wished to leave her clueless on everything. "Stop, please…"

Shizu's eyes looked over to the other's face to finally notice she wasn't looking at her; "Huh?"

"...I'm a stranger, you can't be invested into me..."

"What do you mean?"

"Exactly that, I'm a stranger that you picked up off the street...you do realise that was a stupid move, right?" Ryella could almost feel the chill of the voice's desires repeating inside the back of her mind; it was telling her to *kill.* Clenching her fists, Ryella lowers her head to keep her gaze away from hers. "Shizu, listen to me and listen to me well,"

"I don't understand," confusion and fear brought upon the human woman who just watched as Ryella grab a gun from the drawers near the doorway to the next room, Shizu's face turned pale seeing the unwanted object in her friend's hand.

"Wh-What?"

Face draining of colour, sense of smell become stronger, vision becoming blurry, *I should have told her sooner...it's almost time,* her thoughts continue to remind of what's at stake, she then threw the gun to the human who caught it with a fumble. "Shizu...shoot me right in the heart; there's not much time."

"What? *No*! I won't shoot you!"

"Damn it; you have to!"

In her fear, Shizu had aimed the gun to exactly Ryella had told her, never wanting to make Ryella in rage as much as this, closing her eyes she and hesitantly pulling at the trigger until she heard the noise of the bullet is released. Upon hearing a grunt, she reopened her eyes, for them to meet with, Ryella waving a hand over where the wound would've been but as soon as she moved her hand away Shizu noticed that there was no wound there only a hole in her shirt where the bullet hole meant to be.

The two were silent, for what felt like an eternity, were only for a few minutes until Jen dropped the gun and gasped out; "That... the wounds, the blood and the disappearing act..."

Ryella froze, she felt that voice push its way to the surface, the lust to slaughter the one in front of her almost unbearable, she had to get them away from her; "Shizu run. *Now*!"

"H-Huh?"

"Just run away from here! Now! Please!" Never had Shizu heard her voice sound strained, pained so... split. A scream came out of her lips upon seeing the gun rising very hesitantly. Once seeing that Jen bolted out the front door, her voice strained as she whispered to herself. "Why is this happening now?"

She looked back and regretted it, there she saw Ryella running after her at a record speed gun raised, hair over her eyes and head lowered, but she saw the smirk upon the light-brunette girl's lips. Still, before she knew it, she was on the ground from tripping over, quickly trying to get up but was too late. Panting for air,

Shizu looked up with fear-stricken eyes staring up into violet, a small whimper of fear escaped from her lips which let her 'friend' smirk; "You shall die at the hands of the stranger you picked up, naïve little mortal,"

Shizu kicked Ryella out of the way which gave her the chance to scramble to her feet and run away, but Ryella was on her tail. Lucky enough, or unlucky; however, you see it, Mizuki was out looking for the girl that had disappeared on them while Murasaki was at work. When he came across the screaming and then quickly races to it, this nagging at the back of his mind telling him to.

But when she came across Ryella standing above Shizu. Who had fallen once more with a pistol poised, and was trying to push the barrel from her face.

Mizuki had to think quick, and the only thing that came to his mind was the run over and tackled Ryella before wrestling to get that weapon out of her hands, but not having much luck as she had a vicious grip on that thing. Shizu had moved to the side to desperately watch them while the male yelled for her to run away, but the mortal woman didn't, she waited on frozen in fear.

Mizuki managed to finally get the weapon thrown out of Ryella's grip before he started to throw punches and struggle to make her stop resisting.

Eventually, he was throw off and kicked to the side as she got up and grabbed the gun, aiming it again at Shizu. Only for the dark-haired man to let out a cry as he jumped onto her back, causing them to return to the struggling. Grabbing his arms and attempting to throw him off, they fought for a few minutes before Shizu scrambled over to grab the gun.

Ryella saw and then threw Mizuki off her back finally, and then ran over to the mortal woman, grabbing the gun from her, and making them both fall from the tousle. The pistol finally back in her hand and then aimed at Shizu who stared with tear-stained cheeks and wide eyes in terror.

Ryella smirks with a cackle before; *I don't want this! Please stop!* Is screamed in her mind, cracking the control that was upon her body.

The echo of the bang of that trigger pulled and then dropped from the recoil.

Utau and Murasaki finally had come to Mizuki's call, but their efforts of being there weren't needed anymore.

She stands there staring at her hands in absolute shock, eyes wide as an owl's but vision blurry as if she was underwater. Her voice just croaked out a few sounds before breaking into sobs. The whole area telling her what she had done wrong, only one mistake and it was a fatal one. No one can believe that she did something so vile.

Two others stared down at her, one face white as a sheet and the other with a look of guilt and satisfaction, *Please someone, just tell me it is only just a huge nightmare, that I didn't do this! Not again!* She screams mentally.

"No nightmare compares to the sins you have committed."

"You can never come back for this without running away…"

Hearing Utau and Mizuki's voice, staring at her hands, she erupted into uncontrollable menacing laughter.

Seeing this, the group of friends knew everything for sure.

Murasaki was the first to speak; "Nami, you regained control."

Ryella's laughter halted and stared at her now trembling hands, she then looked down at the girl that laid on her back under here, face pale white, chest heaving from her heavy breaths, and that same look of betrayal and fear. "Only this time…It may not going to stop next time, she may take full control…"

Shizu just stayed staring up at the light brunette's face trying hard to bring something out to say, but all that slipped from her lips was; "You were going to kill me…"

Murasaki, Utau and Mizuki turned to look down at the fear-stricken girl who was trying to get up and away, far away from her mortal friend. Wait, can she even be called that? This so-called friend almost murdered her!

Maybe, she wasn't and was just a burden to her, perhaps she didn't want the friendship and doing this was her way of saying it. So many questions have kept deep down, and new ones surfaced the brink of her mind. Almost going into insanity, tears built up in her eyes on the edge of falling but stayed tamed.

The immortal couldn't look her in the eyes, not after what has witnessed. "I told you to run," was murmured more than said, but Jen heard it, all the same, she was right, Ryella had told her to run, but if so, that means she is unique and couldn't control what happened? "I was trying to warn you," More came out of the immortal while she was looking directly at her, and that statement also answered more of her questions. It was *almost* unavoidable. What happened then was most likely a fluke. "A fluke states it may happen but be worse and vile about it."

It will happen again…?

Ryella saw the look in nineteen-year-olds' eyes and knew what had to be said, carefully getting to her feet, but they all paled hearing sirens nearby. Her eyes widened, but then she dimmed her look turning around; "I'm turning you in whether you like it or not, you're a murderer."

Utau growled hearing that, quickly going over to the dark-brunette and glaring at her; "Do you understand what trouble you're going to get in if you turn her in? Do you realise that we had never fitted in on earth? Do you realise that there are others like her?"

Shizu tried to wrench her arm from the bubble-gum haired girl's grip but she couldn't her strength was unreal, a soft, gentle touch holding the human's arm keeping her from leaving but was harsh to most it away no matter how kind it felt. Shizu slowly turned her head around to face the blue-green eyed immortal; "H-How can you still have a grip on me?"

"Nami, tell her now."

"Déjà vu, that is what I am, and a mere mortal like you will never understand what this means." Tears were rolling down both hers and Shizu's face before Ryella took a deep breath and whispers; *"Restart."*

"Wait, we didn't mean - Nami *don't!*" She overhead Murasaki's voice desperately call out for her to stop, but it was too late, no reload for this world, she couldn't erase everything like that if it were just a reload, she needed to leave the world and to vanish from Shizu's sight in an abundance of glittering dust;

She left.

CHAPTER 13

Sio Region

When Ryella opened her eyes, she would find it to be black of night. Glancing around, she sees that she rests on top of a skyscraper. Slipping to her feet, staggering over to view the city. Or rather, the world that she was now living in.

Clicking her tongue as she thinks back to the last two worlds she was in, Ryella knew that she needed to make a difference. Or at least try to. She couldn't stand this guilt on her conscious anymore. But the whole process of doing so will be another world of hurt if she didn't do it right.

That's when she crossed paths with this pair as they swing past her at top speed, whipping around to watch them run she notices their clothes were a little unusual to what she was used to, but it didn't surprise her. But when she saw one of them suddenly glow in a bright green light, she would hear them call out; "Paint me; Green!"

She was in awe as this young woman suddenly bursts out into pure green energy and then being revealed in this flamboyant pine and a neon green dress decorated in lace and glitter. Along with what looked from afar, to be a long sword from the shimmering silver she could see in the light. Stopping to watch as they went in without fear to fight this glowing white-eyed creature she didn't even see coming until now, she realised just what she could do here in this world.

What kind of good she could do here; Since magic was second nature to some, it seems.

Jolting as the flamboyant female she saw was then tailed by a boy that seemed to have the same powers. A tornado of black, white and midnight lights surrounds him as he also screams out; "Summon the; Dreamland!" as he happens to land just a few kilometres from where Ryella happened to be and then glances to the side as if sensing her presence.

Ryella quickly darts, escaping from being seen so soon, as if they were already out in the night, then they might've realised that she was the cause of an unknown disturbance in their region if they found her that is, "That was close." Now, she was hiding behind the entry the pair she'd been following, had to land in the roof where she was.

It was strange to her, but exciting.

Ryella wasn't sure what she had seen, but by god she was fascinated by it, could humans here actually use magic like that, could she or does the Déjà vu count as her magical ability here? Shaking her head as she moved to approach the pair she saw, Ryella opened her mouth to talk, but they started to speak between themselves instead, so she just ducks back to stay hidden and watch their interaction.

"So, got any more bright ideas?"

"Yeah-Nah, all yours."

They were only two teens, stood together upon a ledge staring down at the brightly lit city in the dead of night, admiring the beauty of the birds' eye view. Her *silver* eyes glanced to the one that stood next to her, a brow raised; "Aw, so no more silly hat tricks, huh?"

She laughed, blonde waves rolling through the wind that pushes pass them, her delicate young features watching the black-haired boy that stood next to her, who began to complain about her unusual laughing at his pain. But that was an average trip for this pair. "All right! I get it! Stop rubbing it in! Thank goodness there are no attacks or we'd be dead right now. We live such a morbid life, my poor sweet Mysterious Rainbow,"

Ryella tilts her head to the side, 'Mysterious Rainbow'? What kind of name was that? She thought to herself before snorting quietly; she had no right to talk, Déjà vu wasn't that much better.

The boy tucked his right ankle behind his left and bowed to her with an arm outstretched, only to jump when a loud static noise, which made them both look down to the pendant around the blonde's neck. "Looks like I have to stop, seems like your time is up,"

"I'll catch you tomorrow night, Nightmare." The blonde girl replies as she leapt off the building to the next.

"That we will, Mistress," before he vanished in the night also.

Which left Ryella moving over into the light to watch them swing/jump around the city away with a smile, she felt that maybe in this world she could. Fit in?

CHAPTER 14

Mysterious Rainbow and Nightmare

Ryella found somewhere to stay for the night, under a shelter near a school but she awoke by the sounds of the students coming into said school, loudly as they're chattering with their classmates.

A tall girl with long blonde hair up in a bun, make up done flawlessly on her face which made her silver eyes stand out, stood out to Ryella. Like she was familiar, but she couldn't work it out on why. Then it hit her, last night that woman on top of the building she saw.

Mysterious Rainbow.

Wait…such a magic user was, just a teenager? What power she had, Ryella was amazed then she moved up over to the woman or instead *tried to*.

Her friend ended up running up, jumping on the fair-haired girl's back and said blonde screech out of surprise. Looking over her shoulder laughing, speaking a morning greeting, "Zephariah, you need to ease up on the shoving; I swear I'm going to kiss the pavement and leave my face imprint one day."

"Amber, my girl, your balance is better than any normal human," a grin was prominent on the other's face as the blonde girl just shoved her away snorting.

Her name was Amber. Amber, huh? A gem name like that matches such a secure magic user like her. Ryella thought, before quickly moving into the school ground over the fence and then to hide before some more significant buildings until all the students vacated.

She was going to talk to this girl, she needed to know how they have such reasonable control over their magic, and she needed to know as soon as possible.

Amber had returned home her classes of the day, but somehow felt this strange feeling she was being watched the whole day and couldn't shake it off.

Tap tap tap.

Amber was inside her bedroom quietly working on her homework and whipped around at the sound, her eyes landing on the sight of the head of Ryella hanging upside down staring into the classroom intently. Feeling a little on edge at sight, and worried, Amber would approach the window and then opening it which let Ryella grab the side and swings her body inside, before straightening up and the grabbing her hands; "You're the one that battled that monster last night! How do you do magic like that? Is it a curse? A gift, what?"

"I-I don't know what you're talking about!"

"Mysterious Rainbow is you! I mean come on, humans are dumb, but I'm not human so! Tell me! How can you transform? Is it a mental thing? Tell me!"

"A-Ah you have the wrong person! There's no way someone that strong could be me!"

Ryella pursed her lips before slowly narrowing her eyes at the blonde girl in front of her before taking a deep breath; "Déjà vu." Amber's eyes widened, which signalled to her that her legacy still is travelled from region to region. But made her wonder just how long had she had this power for? Was she the only one that had that reload button at her disposal? Ah, she was going off-topic. "I see, so my name is known here too…"

"Back off! If you try hurting anyone and then reloading! I-I'll-"

"You won't even remember what I've done to you if I reload, that's the problem."

"H-Huh…?"

"Did you ever think that maybe the Déjà vu wanted to die? Get rid of this cursed power just to live a normal life? To just be human?"

"I-I'm sorry…I-I didn't realise…"

Ryella just rubs her face, mumbling curses to herself before sighing and regaining composure to explain to this girl; "Look, I don't want to keep reloading…You see, I just wish to help people, but worse comes out of it than good."

"Everyone can be a good person if they try."

"I've tried, trust me, that didn't go well."

"So…you have to be the representation of evil no matter what you want?"

"I don't know how this works myself…"

The girls then heard another pair of feet landing onto her porch outside her window and then frowns, Amber, glancing to the taller about to ask something only to be cut off; "Princess, are you – Oh, you have company?" In the form of Nightmare, Nazareth slips through the window only to stare confused at the pair; he's never seen the girl in front of Amber ever before.

"Nightmare, this is…"

Ryella just chuckled before turning to look at the boy before grinning, waving only to take a few steps towards him and pats a hand to his shoulder whispering in his ear; "I'm the Déjà vu if you don't make this timeline worth staying for I might just reload."

"You -" He darts back to stand in front Amber protecting her with an arm, pose ready to fight if he had to, thought Ryella didn't want to fight. "Stay back, don't you dare come any closer!"

"Nightmare, wait! She doesn't mean any harm! She just wants to figure out her true self!"

"No, once evil always evil, with blood staining those hands, who can imagine just how many innocent people she's killed only to return to the same time again to do it again!"

Ryella just stared at them, watching them intently, before sighing heavily, realising she might've taken her joke too far. Closing her eyes, she opened her mouth to say to reload only to be stopped by Amber saying; "Reloading is just running from your problems! Don't reload! Face us, face your demons!"

Her eyes widened at that statement, Ryella knew deep inside that she was right, this girl was smarter than she gave her credit for, a small smile creeping to her face. "Thank you," Ryella then quickly moved to leave the girl's room without another word to them.

CHAPTER 15

Ignorant

The next morning was hell, after getting a lecture from Nightmare, and then waiting for him to leave before she went out for their daily patrol, then homework, she didn't get to sleep that night. But when she came into school greeted by her classmates like usual, but when she reaches her classroom…her day just got worse, Ryella just had to be in her class, sitting at a desk dressed in their uniform and watching her intently. How is she going to deal with the Déjà vu studying with her? "Hey, nice to see you, you listened to me."

"I suppose we got off on the wrong foot too; the name's Stella Armani."

Wait…having her name could prove to be useful to get this woman caught and studied on, to figure out what makes her powers work. Ryella noticed the expression on her face, and could tell what she was thinking, but didn't say anything else about it as Amber's friends came over to her patting her back only to stare at the new face at the desks. At the same time, Nazareth, he ended up narrowing his eyes at her.

She might've taken that little prank a little too far with him. Ryella just sighs before smiling sadly at the look she was given by the boy, but other than that ignored him for most of the day.

When lunchtime hit, Ryella would turn to try and speak to the other mortals in the class but brushed away. They continued on their way, sighing heavily, she would just stay sitting there at the desk, well, until Amber and Zephariah came back into the classroom and walked over, greeting her. Still, to Ryella's surprise, Amber offered her to join them for lunch.

After a while eating, talking between themselves, Zephariah walked off to go speak to someone for a couple of moments, while Amber and Ryella ended up throwing their quite two cents to each other; "Thanks, I didn't expect you to approach me…"

"The fact you showed your face today tells me that you're more human than people give you credit for."

Ryella smiles sadly, playing around with the box that was resting in her lap as she says; "I am human, it's just this *thing* inside me that isn't…I'm trying to stop it…but…it is too strong for me to control."

"Are you saying that it's a sort of *magic* inside you?" Amber was surprised, and confused at the same time before she looks up around at their surroundings then asks when thinking the coast is clear; "Can you elaborate, please?"

So, she did, as quickly and thoroughly as she could. Of what she had been through in the Jitter and Sora region, which made Ryella quite surprised by how much that made sense—listening to every word until a young boy came over to Amber and her while Zephariah was she off somewhere.

"Amber, I see you've made a new friend." Nazareth happened to come over, which made Amber happen to go on guard just a little with the conversation that's spoken about between the two girls, yet, Ryella had already stopped talking when she had heard his footsteps. Though Ryella wasn't the only one hat noticed the somewhat guarded/annoyed expression that he was wearing, Amber did too, but Ryella happened to see something else about him also.

He was that magic-user, Nightmare, wasn't he?

Snorting to herself, Ryella ends up grinning when Amber glances to her and then extends a hand out; "Nice to meet you,"

He took hold of her hand and squeezed it very hard, his eyes fiercely narrowing as he grounded out; "*Likewise.*"

Nazareth's attitude to Ryella. Convinced her this boy in front of Ryella is the partner of Amber next to her. With a snort she pulls his arm towards her, his body falling with it until she could whisper in his ear; "Don't be nasty with me, or I might just reveal that little secret identity of yours to Amber here."

As much as she wanted to stop this sick joke, she felt the strangest urge to continue us just to see this boy's reaction. After all, that returned with a glare, but Ryella just continued with the sick joke she had planned on him either way. He makes the more exciting expressions regarding Amber after all. Ryella snickers before patting his shoulder as she walks past him, leaving the two teens to talk, which she overheard somewhat until she was out of ear range.

"Amber, are you sure you should be associating with her?"

"...I understand, but we have to let at least new people feel welcome, it's common courtesy."

"I know but...you got to remember that this girl is..."

"Oh...so you knew? That makes things easier then, please don't tell Zephariah; she will get too close to study up the mannerisms of her."

"Got it, so just be careful and keep an eye out?"

"Let's just see what she does, yeah."

Of course, they were hostile over her; she can't blame them, after all.

She has murdered people and erased their memories before moving on.

Staring down at her phone of this world, Ryella was confused, how does this *even work*? She always dropped into a world without anything except the clothes on her back. This time, she seems to have some possessions; a phone, in her pocket, and wallet.

Smiling, she would end up approaching Amber and give a peace offering, which was; "I can aid you and Nightmare in finding the source of the magic that is at work."

To say that Amber was surprised that Ryella approached her so confidently and brimming with glee at her idea, Amber sighs; "Fine, we could use someone outside to find out those things."

"Just give me your number, and I'll update you on what information I find okay?"

Since I don't necessarily exist in this world, she wanted to add on but held her tongue on it. Listening as the digits said to her, she would then nod and thank the teen before putting the phone away and being on her way.

Nazareth happened to walk over to Amber, concern on his face before he asks her about what she plans on doing; "Just entertain her until she leaves, then we don't have to worry about her reloading, she'll restart instead."

"If you're sure you can handle this," No, she wasn't sure, because she doesn't know just how strong that bloodlust that Ryella can have, or even…

Just how strong she is altogether.

"I'll handle it, don't worry."

CHAPTER 16

Knowledge

Sighing, Ryella was exhausted, it has been two weeks since she made that deal with Amber, and she had reported to her with little things she found, but she was delighted to help, though when Nazareth was around her staring her down, it made things a little hard to comprehend.

"He wishes that we didn't exist."

Shaking her head rapidly, Ryella tried to remove that voice from her mind so she could focus on the task at hand. Or rather the phone in hand, Ryella had been desperately trying to contact Amber, but to no avail, so she tries her best and moves on to find the female. She was checking back at the school, the teen's home and then the city square.

No sign of her, or rather…no sign of Amber *herself*, she did find Mysterious Rainbow though, with Nightmare surveying the area, Ryella knew she had to think of something, and quickly, otherwise, the information she had will be useless for them.

She knew she couldn't yell that loud, and her phone won't work to contact them, as well as her magic wasn't at the best control point now, either, so eyeing her surroundings, Ryella found out a way to get to their height so she could tell them. That was by climbing an oak tree that was in their view from the roof.

Hurrying; the adrenaline rushing the woman jumps up, grabbing a branch to swing her body and pull herself up. Repeating the process a couple of times, only to see the duo end up swinging their bodies down and across from where they were, which leads to Ryella sitting on the branch sighing miserably at her efforts wasted.

"You know that they are hostile at the mere existence of us, they just accepted it to save their asses. They don't accept you."

Ryella jumped down from the branch she was on, cursing when she felt her knee twist in the wrong direction. Wincing, she sat there for a while as she felt the pain decrease and watched her limb just return to its natural position, and then leapt straight back on her feet, would attempt to call her again, when she didn't get through, Ryella left a message for her to see this time.

After all, those two and their transformations only last for so long; she found out.

When her transformation wore off, Amber stumbled only to hear her phone go off, finally getting the chance to look at it, only to shake her head at the message.

I know who has been doing this, they've been using magic like yours.

God, this girl was ridiculous now. Seriously?

She was getting sick of humouring her, but this was going to be the last time, so Amber quickly sends back;

Did you find out who they were?

Of course, she wasn't expecting a name after all this was all just a sick delusion from the one she is texting.

So when her phone buzzed once more, she was surprised, and even the message itself almost, scare her, no one knew that! So how did she?

Amber, your twin brother, is the source of all the magic. Zane is his name, isn't it?

No one knew of her brother! Not even Zephariah knew. Clutching it hard, she sends back for them to meet up and elaborate, she needed to get to the bottom of this and stop this witch's stupidity.

CHAPTER 17

Repulsive

Ryella read the message once more before looking at her surroundings, ah this was the place. She had to meet Amber to sort this whole black magic thing, she knew. *"She doesn't believe you, she's just going with it, you're just a nuisance in her eyes".* Ryella stopped, once hearing that and thinking to herself, *they were right.* Thinking back to all the times she had told Amber so enthusiastically all the information she had, Ryella remembers, how *bored,* and *exasperated* Amber looked when she *had* spoken to her, even with enthusiasm. *She didn't care*; she didn't also want her alive.

Before she realised, tears were rolling down her cheeks; *"God,* I'm so stupid, thinking that anything can be fixed…"

Wiping her face, she just sends one last message to the woman;

Be warned; the Déjà vu is coming.

She knew the trouble she'll be in when she faces these two.

Amber was going to contact Nightmare to come to find her.

But Ryella was to the stage that she didn't even care, but as they found her, there was a roar from another beast storming around creating havoc. Ryella just stood there watching them as they fought on what to do, going after the monster was decided instead of going after her.

But when it finally came to it, she followed them keeping an eye on the beast more than the two teens fighting it.

When they swing around the being, trying to minimize its movements but to her luck, a familiar feeling weighed her hand down before a smirk slowly crawls onto her face and striking the creature in the leg with the weapon's blade. Through the howling of it trying to remove Ryella from its' leg, said woman darts back with no fear of being hurt in the meantime as her rage reached its peak.

"I will not allow such foolish mortals to humiliate me."

The teen duo was on high alert seeing that wild red eyes followed the bloodlust they could sense, the déjà vu has taken over, and the worse thing about it was they were already struggling with something.

Amber ends up panicking and comes swinging down from the beast, in her last attempts to stop bloodshed anymore, tries to talk Ryella out of her of the oncoming possession that was quickly taking control, "Didn't you want to help? This is *not helping*!"

"Why help someone who doesn't listen to you, huh?"

Amber froze, deer in headlights, she thought she had hidden all how Amber felt about this in the first place down deep that Ryella couldn't see it, but no, she saw *right through* her.

"*Yes, silly mortal, you've been quite* fake *with your interest, so, I'm not going to kill you; instead, you can deal with your brother who is trying to.*"

With a menacing laugh, the beast rips an arm down in its rage, hitting Nazareth out of its way. The body of the human smashing hard against a nearby building; leaving the indent of impact, the splatter of blood under and dripping from him. Slipping agonisingly slow to the unforgiving concrete below and then another limb comes flying towards grabbing Amber. Ryella's face had returned to normal as she stared at the mess of Nazareth in front of her. Glancing back to the struggling teen girl before saying. "It didn't even matter to you the fact I was trying to wash my sins away; instead you chose to ignore it and take the legend, the *rumours* as what I am now, not by what I vouch for for.."

Desperate cries from Amber while she tried to get Ryella to come and help her out of the beast's palms. Ryella just watched on, a blank expression as she continued to speak, the gory scene of human limbs ripped away from the bodies of their owners unfold in front of her. "I'm not reloading, humans like you deserve this torture to learn that all actions have consequences."

Eyes red once more before she laughs; "*Restart.*"

Listening to those bloodcurdling screams as she disappears into another abundance of glittering dust.

CHAPTER 18

Lori Region

Ryella just took a deep breath before opening her eyes to have in her vision a pair blackened eye sockets staring down at hers. Jolting, she had to stare with wide eyes at these creatures that bolted away from her.

Yes, *creatures.* The two men around her were not showing any visible human characteristics besides hands/fingers and general body shape. Though, the one that was seemingly checking on her as she awoke was glowing a bright blue and flickering flame that was his hair flowing behind his head by a hair tie.

What?

"Human? You gave us quite the scare."

Human? Well, she wasn't one either.

Finally, recovering her senses after the initial shock, she quickly glanced around once she realised that she had fallen into another world. Seeing that once again she was in a room, but this one...it was white tiles everywhere. A hospital? No. A lab? "Um...where am I...?" She asks in a timid voice, unsure how to approach speech with these.

Pausing for a second, she realised that her voice came out in a different language it seemed, as she attempted to speak out the words Ryella wanted to ask. When she had to look at the other occupant in the room properly while working out all the questions in her head, one with the body of a human, however, he had slate-coloured skin, dirty blonde hair and big black ram horns. While the other was a human-made up in flames that shone brightly at the sight of her was clad in a black pin-striped button-down, grey vest with a cherry blossom applique on the right shoulder and navy slacks, loosely sitting as he had just finished work.

Furrowing her brow, she was curious about the fact on where she now was, due to the two men, wait are they men? She wasn't sure, maybe speaking to them a little more would help her confusion, they seemed to have been watching over her for a while by the looks on their faces.

So then, what kind of world is this?

"Ah, do no fret human, we won't hurt you." The one made of flames reassured as he bent over to offer a glowing white smile.

"Eugene here brought you to my lab; I haven't had time to look over you,"

The horned creature jerked a thumb to the flaming man, who just ended up grabbing a pair of glasses and slips them over his eyes. "He's been keeping an eye on you."

"I let Lexi know about you, he'll be delighted to know another human has dropped in." Ryella just tilted her head, at the mentioning of another human, but never clarifying whether we're the only odd looking ones or there was more of them. "I have to head back home to my sister, so Herb here, he won't hurt you, but he'll just ask some questions."

Ryella nods and watched the flame being leave before glancing to the other with a tilt of the head. "So, you're a...?"

Herb just snorts at her obvious question, before staring down at her as a pair of white irises shone through the blackened sockets. "Yes, haven't you seen a monster before, kid. You must've lived under a rock."

"Honestly, no, I haven't. Sorry to burst your bubble."

Was he taken aback at the reply? All human knew about them and their kind, how can this human not know. Herb was confused, and he didn't like being confused. "Okay, let me get this straight...you are here, and somehow have never met a monster breed before? You don't seem surprised that you see them now, though."

"I've seen some weird shit in my years; nothing surprises me anymore."

"But you're a kid."

That's when Ryella blinks, confused and curios on what this body has taken the shape of; "Do I look that young...?" She ends up asking him, followed by glancing down at her body to see if she could notice anything, which she just sees a plain olive potato sack of a dress upon what seemed to be a rather short and petite form.

"Well, how old *are* you? And what's your name?" The creature asks raising a brow watching her intuitively.

Ryella had to think quick, furrowing her brow and pursing her lips as she raised her head to look at him, before just giving in and saying; "I don't even know anymore, I've lost track." He seems taken aback from the odd comment and gives her an understanding look; "Let's just say I dropped in unannounced."

He snorts at that one, almost like he could tell the meaning behind it but never said anything about it. "Let's say; you look under twenty then, shall we?"

"Not the first time, so I'll be the judge of that."

He lets out another chuckle at her response before nodding. He helped her up and carefully brought her to a mirror that was nearby int the room to show her what she looked like, Ryella's eyes widened, there stared back a round baby face with tight coils of red hair, and hazel doe eyes stared back in horror of her reflection.

"I-I look twelve!"

"Aren't you, though?" the sarcastic reply held mirth behind those words, gauging her reaction.

Looking to him in the offence, she cries out; "That was rude!" Though deep down she was in slight panic mode at the body, her restart button decided that she would be this age. Ryella turns around to look to the creature with a frown, only to sigh heavily; "Okay, I'm twelve then." He nods, no question asked before grabbing his clipboard and writing some notes down. "…Camilla…my name is Camilla…" When she chose a new name for her new identity that's when everything hits and she just knew that this was another life to live fearing all the same mistakes she had already made.

CHAPTER 19

Introductions

Herb asked her a few more questions before leaving her there in the lab as he was satisfied that she was healthy, no problems from her collapse earlier. He did offer to take her home, well, actually offered to take her to *his* house, since the lab wasn't that far from it.

Ryella felt a little unsure about living with a creature, but it wasn't just her concern but; *The evil voice in her head was worried too.* But ended up agreeing to his terms, Ryella followed him out of the lab as he locked up for the night. Once outside, she would notice it, has been snowing, unusual, she barely has anything on, and it happens to be snowing and freezing when she falls here—remembering for a second that this body was small frail and only clad in a little dress.

Noticing the shivering form Herb just passed her his coat, which she gratefully accepted and slipped it on; "We found you dressed like that,"

"Yes, because undressing a *twelve-year-old* would be the right idea." She was still bitter about her looks age-wise but decided to live with it as Herb laughs at her and offers his hand, which got a glare in return.

"Whatever you say human."

Trudging off with the snow crunching under their feet, they would reach his home, and he would open the door without concern and enters with Ryella following; "I'm home!"

What surprised Ryella more was the fact that a human child was running to them, along with two young-looking versions of Herb, one older than the other as they were holding the other on his shoulders.

They all stopped at the sight of Ryella.

The male human child looked relatively confused at her before shaking their head and introducing themselves. "I'm Lexi! They are Zala and Ashley!" He pointed to each one when he said the names, then grins up at Ryella.

"This is Camilla, and she's *twelve years old*." He made the emphasis on her age which received another glare from the girl before a sigh.

"She has the same Black magic that Lexi uses!"

Wait; what? Who said that?

She looks down to the monster child who was looking up at her with glowing gold irises in those blackened sockets. "Black magic?"

"Yeah, he can heal himself without healing himself and sometimes reloads the timeline."

Ryella widened her eyes before glancing to the human child and then to Herb, who was watching her expectantly. She laughs awkwardly before saying; "I do too. I do have the same time magic as him."

Herb looked a little worried at the confession, but shook his head thinking that they couldn't be, they can just play with time which is better than changing every world in this dimension.

He knew about the Déjà vu landing in this world…but he doesn't believe that it could be this girl next to him.

Ryella felt a little more at ease and moved to talk to those monster children and human child before they would drag her away to show her the house. Herb couldn't only chuckle at how excited they were, and he couldn't wait to tell Eugene in the morning about this.

CHAPTER 20

Timelines

Herb was walking to grab his morning coffee the next day to find the children resting in their beds, except for Ryella who sat at the kitchen table reading some books. The parental creature decided to take the chance to ask the girl some questions; "So, you can reload timelines?"

"Yes, but I only do it if I need to if my existence in their life causes them pain or something to happen to someone, I reload and stay away from them." She replies as honestly as she could, eyes never leaving the book while leaving out the small fraction about the damn voice that controls her actions sometimes too.

"That's awfully kind of you, doesn't it hurt doing that?"

Ryella froze. Feeling all the memories of each timeline she reloads because of what she'd done, all her restarts, mistakes...*everything*. The girl turns to the adult with a sad smile. Other than that, the emotion didn't reach her eyes anymore. "You don't understand how hard it is. I try not to run away from it all, but it makes things worse, so I have to..."

Herbs arms suddenly would wrap around her body and pull her to his ribcage whispering to her; "It's all right, you don't need to reload here..."

"We'll see about that."

He chuckles at her stubbornness as she pulled from his body before looking up at him and smiling, nodding. He then returned to his mission to get that damn coffee before returning to sit with Ryella at the table. "So you don't know how old you are?"

"I don't remember all that much, but from my starting age, which was around...sixteen? I think? So if my calculations are correct, then I'll be around thirty?"

"Wow, my age, huh?"

"Maybe older."

He took a sip and watched her with amusement on his face as she just returned to reading while he threw more questions at her. "Female?"

"As you see,"

"Blood type?"

"I think AB…" She had to pause, unsure as she answered that; *From what I remember back in Jitter, but if it changes with the body then…that's a different issue.*

"Children?"

"No," *Why would I risk the younger generation suffering because of my lack of control?*

"Birthday?"

Ryella froze in surprise before staring at him with her eyes wide as saucers; "I…never had one? I *don't have one*?" That answers his question about the past with family, which would be a possible trigger for the reloads.

There was a slight hesitation as he asked to link up all the information together, "What about your… first, timeline?"

"Ah! Don't you have to go to work? I'll clean up! Don't worry; I'm used to living on my own!"

She pushed the subject away Herb notices, but chose not to question her further about her magic, and merely nodded; "Lexi keeps a phone, if you feel the need at all to reload, either of you, *call me first.*"

Ryella was surprised at how understanding he was about such a thing and the fact that he was …so much, *like a father.*

…Man, he reminds her so much of.

What was his name again…?

Shaking her head, placing his now empty mug over at the sink before grabbing his coast and saying; "Go talk to Ashley or Lexi if you need any clothes and talk to Ashley if Zala acts up."

"Quick question, how old are they?"

"Lexi is eight, Ashley is ten and Zala is three."

"Gotcha, thanks!"

He gave her one last look before quickly bolting out of the house which left Ryella sitting there grinning like an idiot. She felt like she was going to be living with an actual family, time to make a good impression on the kids at least. She moved around and grabbed some things to cook some breakfast for the children.

CHAPTER 21

Proposition

The children all ended up coming down the stairs when they had woken up, Lexi with Zala and then Ashley ten minutes later when Lexi races back up to get him. So Ashley doesn't wake from an alarm.

But when they reached down to the kitchen, they were surprised to see the spread on the table that Ryella had made for them.

"Oh my gosh, you can cook? That's so cool! You have to teach me!" Lexi spoke up before smiling brightly at the female.

"Not a problem, don't reload when you screw up."

"Cami said a bad word!" Zala exclaimed which let Ryella hear the high pitch child's voice that was staring and pointing at her aghast.

Ryella glances down to the others who were looking at her with disapproving looks, and she let out a loud/long exaggerated sigh, she wasn't used to dealing with children, even if she was in a body of one itself; "Just eat."

Lexi just sat down first to try the food, before glancing over and giving an approving look, which told her that she could cook and it tastes fine too.

Ashley, on the other hand, was standing there staring at Ryella as she helped Zala into his high chair to eat as well before their eyes made contact; "You have this…huge case of black magic around you, it's not just your magic…it's *someone else's*. Like the sins are crawling on your back."

Ryella had to shrug it off with a laugh; "Vivid imagination, go eat already." Ryella sat down with them as they ate and then watches Zala make a mess of the food, and she couldn't help but laugh at the antics the toddler got to.

Cleaning him up, she would then blink as the children got themselves ready and moved to the door.

"We've got to go to school now! Thanks for the food, see you tonight, Camilla!"

"Take care of Zala!"

She waves a little surprised at the race out to the school they had to go to. Wait, didn't Lexi have the phone that she meant to use in case of emergencies? She curses, before grabbing and shrugging the squealing toddler on her hip, grabbing the extra serving of food before leaving the house to visit Herb's lab, which she ends up walking into and calling out for the man, Zala helping with his loud squeals of; "Daddy! Food!"

She would giggle at Zala before moving further around each of the rooms to find Herb at the desk with paperwork and whiteboard next to him full of equations and evaluations. "Oi, horn head."

Herb jumps and swings around on his chair before looking confused, only for Ryella to hold up his serve of breakfast, and he seemed grateful for it as he got up to take it off her. "Thanks,"

"Don't expect me to cook you a serving every day."

"Of course not, I appreciate you did though, it looks good." She just smiles before moving to leave only for Herb to grab her free arm and say; "There's something here that you need to be careful of, they are in a shape of anything, they travel from world to world. The Déjà vu has entered our world, and we need to all be careful."

That's all was being said as Ryella stood there watching the man while Zala squealed; "Deba bu!"

Herb sighed; "Sorry, that was…too much for a kid to know, huh?"

"…Do you have any information on the Déjà vu…?"

That surprised him that she asked such a thing, watching as she slowly moves to kneel on the tiled ground placing Zala down on her lap.

"I know a little…what did you want to know?"

"Is there… Is there a possibility that the Déjà vu is a spirit, inhabiting a human vessel…?"

"It is, I believe that the human has shown compassion too many times not to want to be a part of the slaughter, but has a lack of control on the Déjà vu…"

"Have you…seen the vessel then…?"

Herb paused before glancing over to the whiteboard and then sighing, he grabs his child before looking to her; "This may explain more than my words, follow me." She made no complaints and followed the man into a hidden room down in the basement of the laboratory. She was stepping into the darkroom when he clicked a switch and watched the light brighten up the room—staring around at the giant screens that decorated the wall dead ahead and then the computer desk with more resting upon it.

But what scared her *was the screens showed her most recent restarts.*

He has been studying the Déjà vu for a long time, but…how could he be able to see things in different worlds? Had he made something that could move?

Shaking her head, she listened to him when he went up to the screen and quickly typed up something and says; "This is where the Déjà vu vessel showed the most amount of emotion like she was fighting something that was inside her."

Looking to the screen once more, she would see the clip of her and Shizu.

No…why did he have to remind her of that night? How she *almost* killed that naïve woman that only wanted to be a friend of hers. The sight of her fight with her mental stability was another thing. Ryella was hardly able to say anything; it was all a shock to see this.

"He sees all your sins; he knows what you've done…"

And Ryella freaked out, eyes widening before she had to step away slowly. "No. No, no, no. This isn't working, I-I have to g-get…"

Herb realised she was having a panic attack and raced down to the knee in front of her, hands on top of hers and holding them tightly in his cold yet gentle claws; "Breathe Camilla. *Breathe.*"

She tried to control her breathing before little Zala reaches up to smack his hands on her cheeks, making her look down to that focused little face. "Bweeve!"

Ryella let a small smile creep to the surface before letting out a sigh and looking straight back up to Herb nodding, his hands never moving from hers. "Camilla, did you have experience with the Déjà vu before you collapsed…?"

Thank god for him asking that because that's how she can cover up the fact of her being the Déjà vu. "Y-Yeah…I guess she's like the legends say…huh? Merciless."

"He will find out eventually…"

Her breath hitched again, and she tightened her grip against Zala, which lead to the child looking up confused.

"I rest by what I say; we are not like her; we will take care of you. Like you were my daughter." Once again, relief flooded her system, and she closes her eyes, slipping from consciousness and falling to her side with Zala wailing at sight and being in her arms.

Black, that's all she saw, taking small steps in the black, she would soon break out into a run, desperately searching for something within the darkness.

"How could they?"

She stumbles, losing her footing and was falling into the endless black, looking up, she sees a silhouette in the darkness. It was materialising in front of her, falling with her to give her a knowing, creepy grin. Ryella ends up jerking her head away from the thing as it materialised into a spitting image of her.

"Watch them burn."

Shaking her head, trying to rid the thought, the *sight* in front of her; "I don't want this! You're not me! Who are you?"

"I am you, your desires that you keep deep down."

"No, you aren't! I never wanted to *kill* anyone!"

The doppelganger then reaches out to grab her shoulders tightly enough to make her wince from the grip; *"Betrayal, fear, loneliness. These are all the mortals have done to you..."*

"Everything goes tits up because of the magic you possess!"

A hand slips away from the tight grip to gently caress Ryella's face that now was full of fear, *"This is what those monsters want, you to love them and trust until the last moment when they will split your heart and soul apart... I will stop that."*

Ryella felt her airways closing, struggling to breathe as the figure in front of her swirled into a mass of black once more and crept over Ryella's from swallowing her whole.

"I will make everything end soon."

Ryella woke up screaming, bolting up from the bed and look around in panic before she ran out the bedroom door met with a worried Herb who was about to grab the doorknob in a fear. "Camilla? Whatever is the matter? Are you okay?"

She just ran straight into his chest not saying any words but gripped the shirt he wore sobbing hard. He just stares down at her form patting her back glancing down the stairs at the worried children watching him followed by Eugene walking up the stairs in concern, well, as much interest as his bright flaming face could express.

"Is she okay?"

"Probably a nightmare,"

"I never thought the Déjà vu attacked children; we haven't even seen any movements from her yet..."

"You can't keep me a secret for too much longer."

Ryella froze up when hearing that, slowly she pulls away to glance over to Eugene only for her to open her mouth to say something. But she was cut off before the words formed when Ashley came running up the stairs, pushing past Eugene and hugging her, Herb looked down at them with a smile before saying; "We were all worried about you, Camilla, thank you for not…reloadting…" Ryella just nods before wrapping her arms around the skeleton child who was the same height as her before she heard in her ear; "You can't lie to me about what you are, just because dad can't see it doesn't mean no one can't…"

She stiffens up when she heard that, feeling all blood drain from her face at that. *A child knew about the Déjà vu inside her.* She was so close to freaking out, but she couldn't while Eugene and Herb were still there.

Once they finally decided to walk back downstairs, Ryella shoves Ashley away from her with panic flaring in her eyes. "Pl…Please don't tell them…"

"I won't say anything as long as you do something for me." She was confused but agreed, listening to what she had to do. "You can't let anyone else find out, but we can work together on this. Tell me everything about the Déjà vu."

"Huh…? You want to help me…?"

"Because…I've seen the relationships the human vessel has made…the warnings she gave to the humans that were near her when the Déjà vu was going to take over…"

"…The deal, you don't tell your dad, and I'll explain everything I can." She can't believe she just made a deal with a ten-year-old monster with this world at stake—what a new low for her.

CHAPTER 22

Target

Ryella ended up in the region for five years, which left her in a very frustrating time of two pubescent teens, one a monster and the other human male. And things were becoming quite…*awkward*.

Herb noticed Lexi make the first move only just turning shy from fourteen and he was already throwing sexualised jokes to Ryella which makes Ashley crack up and Herb scold him while Ryella just covers Zala's precious ears with a sigh. "Puberty is the worst."

"You would know, you've gone through it about ten times." Ashley gave her a cheeky grin with that glowing green tongue sticking out, which he's been doing recently much to the female human's annoyance.

How the hell can you control a monster going through puberty?

That question was never getting answered by Herb that's for sure.

Ryella just sighs miserably at their immature behaviour and thanking God that Zala was still only a preteen which made her happy. However, Ashley was mature enough to keep her identity even a secret, which made her feel grateful to the teenage creature, but this was ridiculous. Ryella looks to Herb who was racing against time again for work; she realises she'll have to make lunch for him and take it over the back today.

Ashley and Lexi were already in their uniform ready for school, which Ryella refused to go to, and she teaches Zala at home. After these years Ryella got given her phone to call Herb if need be but ended up calling Ashley whenever those dark urges came up which was rare now.

But as much as things were going reasonably steady now, she still was cautious about things.

She didn't want anything to ruin the lifestyle that she had created. Ryella watched Zala as he was at the table writing on the worksheet that she had written out for him.

When she heard the door knocked on, she went to answer it, expecting Eugene to drop by like he usually does.

But it wasn't, the one standing there was …a robot? There were robots in this world? She was confused until here was n arm blaster aimed straight at her face. Ryella knew what came next and ducked just as it

66

was triggered hyper glowing beam bursting through and hitting the sofa burning it.

Hearing Zala screaming, Ryella grabs the child and throw him across the room to the back door; "Go! Hurry! Get Ashley or your father!"

Rolling around as he landed out in the snow and stumbled to his feet to take two steps back crying out; "C-Cami!"

Only to be stopped by the returning voice. "*Go!*"

As he stumbles back to his feet, the skeleton child ran out the door as more blasts were heard through the house, even one breaking through a wall and just missing Zala which caused him to be startled and start crying.

But he knew the mission he was given and hurried to find his brothers.

Zala finally reached the school and desperately ran through the school ground. Frantically ran through the school ground with his tired little body slipping between students until he was caught by the arm and see the face of Lexi who was kneeling trying to get the child to calm down and speak.

"Zala? What are you doing! Where's Camilla?"

"C-Cami – Blaster! H-Hurt!"

He couldn't form a proper sentence with the way he was crying, but Lexi grabbed his phone to hurry and call Ashley; "You have to go home right now! Zala is with me, and he's distraught! Something has happened to Camilla too, check on her! I'm on my way too!" He didn't wait for a response, Lexi just moves out of the school grounds holding Zala in his arms before trying to ease the child down.

Hoping Ashley would get there in time.

"Target located, elimination in progress."

Ryella was desperately trying to dodge all the blasts thrown her way, but it was getting harder and harder when that little voice in her was coaxing her with sweet little words to;

"*Destroy threat; it must die for attempt…*"

Ryella felt a lump in her throat; she couldn't; she won't destroy this being in front of her.

She can't.

One more time a blast came out and this time she didn't move out of the way quick enough and got a hit in the chest with it, causing a massive amount of blood to flow pouring from the open hole and splashing on the ground, before flopping over.

"Reload, Reload."

But she was too stubborn to bother saying it, or even letting the reload evident her wounds. Still, it did, slowly loading her body to her perfect health, it stopped halfway as Ashley finally teleports into the house, but he had grabbed Herb as well, and he stared at the scene as Ashley raced to her yelling; *"Reload*! Camilla let the 'Reload' heal you!"

Herb was staring at the robot that was now lowering his blaster as he saw the parental monster only for it to say; "Target located;"

"Stand down."

Ashley would hold Ryella to his body, desperately trying to force her to use her powers only for Herb to come over and push his son out of the way.

"Is she the Déjà vu?"

Herb left the girl where she was only to stare down his son, covered in the blood of the evil disguise, frantic. Ashley refused to say, he only stared at him trembling with his eye sockets full and glowing irises; "I promised n-not to tell you! But she – Camilla is human! She doesn't want to live if it causes others harm! Can't you see? The Déjà vu is *something* that *controls* her!"

"You should have told me in the first place, Ashley!"

"I couldn't! I didn't want to make her reload!"

"She could've *killed* you or Zala! Didn't you even think of that?"

"I did, I'm not that stupid dad! I knew the possibilities! Couldn't you see how much she was struggling?"

He looks down to the fallen girl who was moving sluggishly to look over to the father of the monsters. "Why isn't she reloading…?"

"Because she refused to prove that she is the Déjà vu, she rather dies, then shows she was…"

"Why is she trying so hard to keep it a secret?"

Ryella just slowly gets up, the hole in her chest forcefully but still quite slowly healing over; her head lowered as she got her balance back. He took a step back and guarded Ashley with blue irises glowing. "Because my vessel here wanted to have a family to fit in. But no one would accept her and who she was, who accepts her even with her sins." She raised her head to look at Herb and Ashley with one red-eye and one regular, that half-crazed expression and half saddened/lifeless. "She is a strong vessel but emotionally weak. I took it upon myself to make her feel at ease. But as we moved to different worlds, that defiance and refusal or my behaviour for her."

Herb narrowed his eyes, realising that everything that he had said clicking in his head how everything about an evil spirit taking over her was causing every issue in the world.

"By the third Restart, she wanted to save the worlds instead of destroying it for messing with her," Ashley finally came back to his feet and watched them, or rather the Déjà vu speak them. "But you, you made my vessel feel like she was a part of a family, but only one of you accepted her sins."

"But…What *are* you?"

"That's an excellent question, but unfortunately I have no answer for that either…but you have no choice but to accept this."

Ashley ended moving closer to her, which lead to Herb trying to stop him and ended up having his son standing inches from the woman. "Please don't force Camilla to kill anyone anymore. Please don't force her to do what she doesn't want; we will all accept both of you if you guarantee that."

"Mistreat her, lie to her; *I will kill you.*"

That crazed look soon disappeared from the side of her face, and her head hung low before slowly rising back up and wincing; "…God…that smarts…"

Ashley was looking at her in amazement before he just smiles and cracks up laughing. "You two are something…"

Ryella gives him a sheepish smile only to suddenly enveloped in a pair of arms in a rush. Knocking the wind out of her before glancing down to the young teen monster. Nothing was said, until Herb came over looking at them sternly, almost glaring down at the two before saying; "Next time warn me if the psychopath that travels through worlds is living under my roof so I can prepare *not* to have my house ruined by Tracker."

Ryella looks over to Herb and just stares at him; "You know all along didn't you…?"

"I had a small hunch…"

"I am so sorry…"

"Ashley is right though; you are a part of this family, *both* of you."

Ryella felt relief flood her system, the voice in her head was quiet, no complaints, no taunts, nothing.

She was at peace.

And it was with this family.

When Lexi finally arrived with Zala after he got him to calm down only to stare at the destruction that was their home and tilts his head at the three that were sitting in the middle of mess talking. "What did I miss?"

Ryella and Ashley looked over to the pair before cracking up laughing and ended up explaining what was going on.

EPILOGUE

Weeks later, once the house repairs started with Eugene's help, much to the large lecture and a thorough explanation, the family just stayed with Eugene until the house finished. Then it came to this moment; Lexi and Ashley were standing with Ryella ready for a mission they knew was bound to happen; "Are you sure you want to do this?"

"I need to. I need to set the timelines right."

Herb just smiles at her, giving her an embrace before leaving his hands resting on her should, before looking to Ashley and Lexi. "Are you sure you two are okay with this?"

"She said the spirit told her it'd work, but it's not a restart. More like a load to save point."

Lexi and Ashley soon give him a brief embrace.

"If you're worried, you can contact us through Tracker."

He nods, feeling more at ease before Ryella grabbed his children's hands; "Herb, the spirit told me to tell you," She pauses when the parental monster turns to meet her eyes, "My real name is; Ryella Teiran."

And she disappeared, and the boys disappeared into an abundance of glittery dust while Herb watched them go looking like a proud father.

"Huh. What a fitting name."

"So, who are finding first?"

"Wow, this world is bright…"

Ryella just laughs as their excitement to the new world they had landed, saying; "Meet the *Sio* region."

Printed in the United States
By Bookmasters